The Boxcar Children are helping endangered animals!

The Aldens watched three beluga whales swim through the tank. One came close by to peer at them. Its mouth seemed to be smiling.

"They are so cute!" Violet called, moving closer to get a better look.

The Aldens' guide, Kayla, leaned her elbows on the railing. "They sure are," she said. "I love coming to the aquarium to see the whales. But we can't forget about the animals that aren't as popular or as cute. All species are important."

"Every animal should be protected," Henry agreed. "Not only the biggest or cutest ones. I'd like to know how to help those other animals too."

The other children nodded.

Kayla smiled. "I have just the idea. But we'll have to leave the aquarium. Are you ready for a new adventure?"

S0-BCS-855

CREATED BY
GERTRUDE CHANDLER WARNER

BOOK 1

The Big Spill Rescue

ALBERT WHITMAN & COMPANY
CHICAGO, ILLINOIS

Copyright © 2022 by Albert Whitman & Company
First published in the United States of America
in 2022 by Albert Whitman & Company

ISBN 978-0-8075-1016-2 (hardcover)
ISBN 978-0-8075-1017-9 (paperback)
ISBN 978-0-8075-1018-6 (ebook)

All rights reserved. No part of this book may be reproduced or transmitted in any
form or by any means, electronic or mechanical, including photocopying,
recording, or by any information storage and retrieval system,
without permission in writing from the publisher.

THE BOXCAR CHILDREN® is a registered trademark
of Albert Whitman & Company.

Printed in the United States of America
10 9 8 7 6 5 4 3 2 1 LB 26 25 24 23 22 21

Illustrations by Craig Orback

Visit The Boxcar Children® online at www.boxcarchildren.com.
For more information about Albert Whitman & Company,
visit our website at www.albertwhitman.com.

CONTENTS

CHAPTER 1

Help Needed

"I want to touch a shark!" called six-year-old Benny Alden.

"Shh!" Benny's sister Jessie put a finger to her lips. "The sign says we should whisper."

Benny put his hand to his mouth. Then he whispered, "I want to touch a shark!" just as excitedly, but quieter.

The Aldens were at the Port Elizabeth Aquarium. In front of them, a shallow tank stretched across the room. Inside, small sharks and stingrays swam lazily among rocks and plants. A sign above read Touch Tank. That meant visitors were welcome to reach into the tank through the open top.

Grandfather put his hand on Benny's shoulder. "You'll get a chance, but first we have to learn the rules."

"That's right," said Isaiah Young. "Listen to Kayla. She'll explain."

Mr. Young was an old friend of Grandfather's. The Aldens were staying with him while they visited Port Elizabeth. Kayla, his daughter, was their un-official guide to the aquarium.

"Thanks, Dad." Kayla spoke softly. "We whisper so we won't frighten the animals. You should also move slowly. Put your hand right under the surface of the water. Hold it there with your palm down."

Kayla wore a blue collared shirt and had black hair that hung down to her shoulders. She was a biologist and knew all about the animals they were going to see at the aquarium. It was clear she knew what she was talking about, and some other visitors even gathered around to listen.

The four children followed Kayla's lead. A stingray swam toward them. As it rose in the water, Violet's hand stroked across its back. She tried to keep quiet but let out a tiny squeal of joy and excitement. "It's smooth and slippery," she said.

"It didn't touch me," Benny said sadly.

"Be patient," Grandfather said.

"Are there other rules?" Jessie asked. She was twelve and liked to make notes about everything she learned. She couldn't write in her notebook with her hand in the water, but she'd try to remember what she learned for later.

"Don't try to grab the animals," Kayla said. "And don't try to touch their bellies or tails. Instead, touch their backs."

"What happens if you touch a shark's tail?" Benny asked. "Will it bite?"

Kayla smiled. "These sharks won't bite. There are

about four hundred species of sharks in the world, and most are small and gentle, like these. You can handle them easily."

"We still need to treat them with respect," Henry said. At fourteen, he was the oldest of the Alden children.

"That's right," Kayla said. "We should treat all animals with respect. Here at the touch tank, the sharks and rays will hide if you scare them. But if you are calm and gentle, they'll get curious and come out."

"I don't want to scare them," Benny said. "I want to make friends."

Benny held his hand under the water. His body wanted to squirm, but he tried to stay very still. A speckled shark as long as his arm swam toward him. Benny held his breath. The shark nosed at his hand, and Benny got nervous. Then it slid past, letting Benny pet down its back.

"I touched one!" Benny grinned and clapped his hands together. Water from his wet hand sprayed into his face. He wiped himself off with his shirt sleeve as the other children laughed quietly.

After a few more minutes at the touch tank, Kayla asked, "Shall we move on?"

Everyone agreed. They were excited to see the other animals at the aquarium. After the children had washed and dried their hands, Kayla led the way to the next room.

Violet walked beside her. "We don't get to touch wild animals very often," she said. "I've been to a petting barn at the zoo, but those animals aren't wild." Ten-year-old Violet loved animals. She hoped she'd get a chance to draw some during their visit to Port Elizabeth.

"You shouldn't touch animals in the wild," Kayla said. "It can be dangerous. They could hurt you, or you could hurt them. The aquarium chooses animals that are safe for the touch tank, and the tank gives them places to hide if they feel shy. The workers also keep the tank clean and watch for any sign of disease."

"That sounds like a lot of work," Violet said. "Why not let people look but not touch?"

"Good question," said Kayla. "Many people are afraid of sharks and rays, but here they see these animals aren't so dangerous. Maybe after this, your little brother will fall in love with sharks. Maybe he'll become a shark researcher someday."

"I could do that!" Benny said. "I already made friends with that speckled one."

They made their way into a glass tunnel. On the other side of the glass, water filled a huge tank. It felt like they were underwater with the fish! This tank held larger animals. Some of the fish were as long as a person was tall. At the bottom, crabs scuttled between sea urchins and coral.

Violet pointed through the glass. "Oh, that one is pretty. It looks like an orca, but it's too small. Is it a baby?"

"That is a Hector's dolphin," Kayla said.

The dolphin was mostly black. It had white from its chin down its belly. The black-and-white pattern had reminded Violet of an orca, which she knew was the largest member of the dolphin family.

"Hector's dolphins are the smallest marine dolphins

in the world," Kayla said. "They are very rare and very endangered."

Benny frowned. "Are they in-dangered from people?"

"The word is *endangered*," Jessie said.

"Endangered means a species is at very great risk," Kayla said. "Only about seven thousand Hector's dolphins still live in the wild. If we don't help them, they might all die out. Then they would be all gone—extinct."

"That's awful," Benny said.

"Don't worry, Benny," said Henry. "Lots of people help protect animals. Right, Kayla?"

"That's right!" Kayla said. "There are many conservation groups that help. I work for one called Protectors of Animals Worldwide, or PAW."

Violet watched the dolphin as it swooped through the water. It swam close to the glass. Then it turned on its side, flicked its tail, and zipped away. It circled back around and wiggled as it passed by once more.

"It's dancing!" Benny said. He went up to the glass

and started wiggling, trying to copy the dolphin's moves.

"You called this a marine dolphin," Violet said. "Marine means it lives in the ocean, right?"

"That's right," Kayla said. "Most dolphins live in the ocean, but a few live in rivers."

Benny spun around. "Will we see one of these dolphins in the ocean?"

"I don't think so." Kayla smiled. "Hector's dolphins live near New Zealand."

"That's on the other side of the world," Henry explained.

Benny sighed. "That's a long way. Maybe someday we can go."

"That would be quite an adventure," Grandfather said.

"I like adventures!" Benny raised his arms over his head as a sea turtle swam up to the glass. It looked like it wondered what Benny was doing. "We've had a lot of adventures," Benny told Kayla.

"Oh really?" she asked.

"It's true," Henry said. "We like to help people and solve mysteries."

"We like to help animals too," Violet added.

"I try to help animals," Kayla said. "I don't think I've ever solved a mystery though."

Benny smiled up at her. "That's okay. Maybe we'll find one for you while we're here."

Kayla laughed.

Grandfather said, "Don't be surprised if it happens. My grandkids always find something to get into."

The Aldens' adventures had started when the children ran away from home. After their parents had died, they'd heard their grandfather was mean, so they hid in the woods and lived in an old boxcar they found. That had been their first adventure. Then they met their grandfather and found out he was very kind. He brought the children to live with him in Greenfield, Connecticut. The children still liked to hang out in the boxcar—and they still had plenty of adventures.

Benny skipped through the room. "Maybe someday I'll get to travel all over the world. I'll see animals and help them."

"Those are very good goals," Kayla said.

Jessie pulled out her notebook. "Can you tell me more about conservation? It means trying to protect nature, right?"

Kayla nodded. "PAW has programs around the world. We try to save animal species, and that means we have to protect the land. After all, you can't protect animals if they don't have a safe and healthy place to live. Everything in nature is connected."

"What do you mean?" Benny asked.

"Say a factory dumps chemicals onto the ground," Kayla said. "The chemicals can wash into a river. They can flow into lakes or all the way to the ocean. What happens if you drop a plastic bag outside? It might blow miles and miles to the coast. It could get into the water and choke a sea turtle or seal."

"That's terrible," Violet said.

"We're always careful to throw away our garbage," Henry said.

"That's important," Kayla said. "Environmental

groups like mine try to educate people on things like that. We work with local communities. We work with governments. Like I said, everything is connected. People are part of that web."

Violet looked back at the dolphin and drew in her sketchbook. It was hard to draw something that moved so quickly. "I hope more people come and see animals like the Hector's dolphin," she said.

"Many people love dolphins," Kayla answered. "Most people don't know about all the different dolphin species. They don't realize some are so rare they might disappear forever. Aquariums help teach people about all the animals in danger."

"It's sad that there are so many of them that need help," Violet said, putting down her pencil.

Kayla put her hand on the girl's shoulder. "It is sad. But isn't it nice that people want to help? Come on to the next room. We'll meet another species. This one is really *cool*."

Benny dashed ahead. "Penguins!"

In the next room, penguins played in a large area

behind glass. They waddled across rocks and dove into a pool of water. Through the glass, visitors could see them swimming underwater. Violet plopped down cross-legged. She held her sketchbook in her lap and drew.

"The aquarium has African penguins and rockhoppers," Kayla said. "These are the African penguins. Rockhoppers have funny yellow feathers on their heads."

"They're adorable," Jessie said. "Are they endangered?"

"Sadly, yes," Kayla said. "Of the eighteen species of penguin, ten are endangered. Others are vulnerable. That means they aren't endangered yet, but there aren't as many as we'd like. Rockhopper penguins are vulnerable. African penguins are endangered."

The group spent some time watching the penguins, then Kayla led them outside, where a railing surrounded a huge pool. Inside were the biggest animals yet. "These are beluga whales," Kayla said. "They are found around Alaska and other northern areas."

The Aldens watched the three pale-gray whales swim. One came close to peer at them. It had a bulging, rounded forehead. Its mouth seemed to be smiling.

"I thought whales were really, really big," Benny said.

"These are one of the smaller whale species," Kayla said.

Jessie read the sign. "They're still eleven to fifteen feet long. That's twice as long as Grandfather is tall, and the adults weigh more than one thousand pounds!" She made notes.

"I bet they have to eat a lot." Benny rubbed his stomach. "Like me."

"They are so cute!" said Violet.

Kayla leaned her elbows on the railing. "They sure are," she said. "I love coming to the aquarium to see the whales. But we can't forget about the animals that aren't as popular or as cute. All species are important."

"Right." Jessie looked up from her notebook. She thought she understood what Kayla was saying now. "Like you said, we are all connected. Bees pollinate many foods we eat. Snakes eat mice that would eat farmers' grain. Some people don't like bees or snakes, but we need those animals too."

"Every animal should be protected," Henry agreed. "Not only the biggest or cutest ones. I'd like to know how to help those other animals too."

The other children nodded.

Kayla smiled. "I have just the idea. But we'll have to leave the aquarium. Are you ready for a new adventure?"

"Always!" Benny said. "But maybe lunch and then an adventure, okay?" He rubbed his stomach again. "I'm hungry!"

CHAPTER 2

A Day at the Beach

After lunch Grandfather and Mr. Young left to go catch up on old times. Kayla took Henry, Jessie, Violet, and Benny to the Port Elizabeth waterfront. They walked along docks, where shops looked out over the water. Wooden piers on thick pillars stretched out into the ocean. Some piers had small boats pulled up to them. Others had people fishing or taking photos.

Benny jumped from board to board on one of the piers. He liked the way the wooden boards bounced a little every time he landed.

"Watch out!" a fisherman called out. The man wore an orange life preserver and a flat-brimmed cap.

Benny stopped. He hadn't been very close to the man. He wasn't going to bump him or his fishing gear. Still, Benny said he was sorry.

Henry stood next to his brother. "He didn't do anything wrong."

"Well, maybe not." The man lifted his cap and pushed back his blond hair. "I guess I was afraid the bouncing might make my fishing pole fall." The man had a patch of sunburn on his nose. Benny noticed his burned nose almost matched his orange life preserver.

Kayla and the girls gathered around. The man held out his hand to Kayla. "I'm Austin Green. I've seen you around."

Kayla introduced herself and shook his hand. Then she introduced the children.

Benny looked at all the man's gear. A fishing pole

leaned against the wooden railing. A big tackle box sat at the man's feet. It was open, showing hooks and fishing line. A closed cooler sat next to it.

"You have a lot of fishing stuff," Benny said.

"I have a lot more than this," Austin said. "That's my boat over there." He pointed to a blue fishing boat tied to the pier.

Benny tilted his head. "Your boat is blue, but your name is Green. You should have a green boat."

"Well, I like the color blue," the man said.

"I would call that navy blue," said Violet. "That's a good color for a boat, Benny. The Navy goes out to sea."

Benny tilted his head the other way. He hadn't thought of that.

"If you have a boat, why are you fishing here?" Henry asked. Henry motioned to the man's life preserver. He thought it was strange Austin was wearing it on shore. "Are you going out soon?"

Austin looked down. "Oh this?" He looked a little embarrassed. "No, I guess I wear it out of habit. Port Elizabeth is having a big striper fishing tournament right now."

"What's that?" asked Benny.

"Striped bass," said Austin. He led the Aldens to a sign nearby. "The tournament is a shoreline fishing competition. No fishing from boats. That helps make it an even playing field for everyone. When I win I'll prove I'm the best fisherman in town."

An older man standing by the sign chuckled. He had a fishing pole with a line in the water. "Wait until you make it to the top of this leaderboard before you start bragging. You've never won before."

"Well, I have to work!" Austin said. "I'm not retired like you. I can't stay out fishing all night like you can."

"People go fishing at night?" asked Violet.

Austin nodded. "That's when the striped bass are most active." He turned to the old man. "If I could stay out all night fishing, I would win for sure. But this will be my year anyway. You'll see."

The older man shrugged. "I'll believe it if I see it." The man headed off to go fishing.

Kayla talked with Austin for another minute about the competition. She was curious about how many fish were being caught. As the two talked, the Aldens watched boats come and go.

Violet pointed out over the water. "Look at that one," she said. "It doesn't look like the others."

"Most of these boats are fishing boats," said Henry. "But that one has a rounded front. It doesn't look like it's made to go fast. It has a big cabin though."

The boat captain must have seen them watching. She waved and gave a friendly smile. The children waved back.

When Kayla was done talking to Austin, the group continued down the docks and onto the beach. As they walked a nice breeze blew off the ocean. It smelled sort of fishy.

"It's quieter here," Violet said. "Peaceful."

"Yes," Jessie agreed. "I'm surprised there aren't more people on the beach. I guess it's only May. Maybe it gets more crowded later in the summer."

"Most people stay closer to town," Kayla said.

"That's good. You'll see why in a minute."

In the distance the flat beach changed as low hills sprung up into dunes. The children spotted a sign ahead. When they got closer, Henry could read it. "'Beach closed to vehicles,'" he read.

"How can you close a whole beach?" Benny asked.

"It means vehicles like cars are not allowed to go any farther," Henry said.

"I wouldn't drive on the beach anyway." Benny jumped in the sand. "It's more fun to walk. The ground is squishy."

Henry read more of the sign. "It says there is a protected animal habitat ahead."

"Ooh, what kind of animal?" Violet asked.

Before anyone could answer, an engine roared. It got louder and louder, making a whining sound. A red-and-black all-terrain vehicle came down the beach. Sand flew up from behind the wheels. Kayla hurried toward it, waving her arms.

The ATV turned and skidded to a stop, spraying sand across Kayla's legs. The driver wore a red-and-black helmet to match the ATV. She pulled off the helmet and her long brown hair spilled out.

The woman said her name was Jenny Mitchell. "What's the problem?" she asked.

"The beach is closed here," Kayla said. "You can't take your vehicle any farther."

Jenny blew out a loud breath. "It's so annoying!" She explained that she had been off-roading all around the world. "I came to Port Elizabeth because the sand dunes are supposed to be so awesome. But I'm not allowed to go anywhere!"

Kayla crossed her arms. "We have to protect the beaches."

Jenny also crossed her arms. "Who are you, the nature police?"

"I work for Protectors of Animals Worldwide," said Kayla. "So basically, yes." She pointed at the sign. "In any case, you can see the rules."

"All right, fine!" She grumbled as she headed back to her ATV. "I'll have to find another way to make this lousy place interesting. Maybe I'll try riding at night." She jammed her helmet onto her head and sped back the way she came.

Kayla glared after her. Finally, the ATV vanished from sight.

"She didn't seem very nice," said Benny.

"No, she didn't. It's a good thing this is here." Jessie tapped the sign saying the beach was closed. The sign tipped to one side. "Whoops."

"It's not easy to keep this upright in sand." Kayla straightened the sign. She still looked concerned about the woman on the ATV. Then she brightened up. "Let's keep going. We just might get to see the protected animals."

"What are they?" Violet asked.

Kayla just smiled. "You'll see."

Benny skipped ahead. "Maybe we can guess. Maybe we're going to see...a huge whale! One of the really big ones."

"I don't think they would close the beach for a whale," Henry said. "The whale would stay in the ocean."

"What about a sea turtle?" Violet asked. "They come to shore sometimes."

Benny ran back to Kayla. "Is it a turtle? Did we get it right?"

"No turtles and no whales." Kayla pointed ahead. "Here we are."

A low fence stretched across the beach. It was made of up of small wire squares. Behind the fence the sand rose into dunes.

"I don't see anything," Jessie said.

"Nothing?" Kayla asked.

"Well…" Jessie shaded her eyes against the sun. "I see sand dunes and some grass and wildflowers. I see some insects in the grass. That's all." She cocked her head. "I do hear something though. What's making that sound?"

They heard short, high-pitched whistles. Just then a little bird ran past on the sand. It had a pale gray back and a white breast. A ring of black ran around its neck. It almost blended into the sand behind it. Only the orange on its beak and legs stood out.

"A little birdy!" said Violet.

"That is a piping plover," Kayla said. "And this is its nesting ground."

Benny giggled. "Piping plover, piping plover. That's fun to say."

The bird moved in quick little darts, a few steps at a time. It grabbed something in the sand with its beak.

"It must be eating bugs." Benny made a face. "Yuck." He liked almost every kind of snack, but not bugs! The birds could keep those.

Another plover joined the first one.

"They're so small," Jessie said. "Each one would fit in my hand. I'd like to hold one."

"Give it a better snack than bugs," Benny suggested. "Maybe it will come to you."

"We have to keep our distance," said Kayla. "This pair is getting ready to mate. Then they'll nest. Hopefully there will be babies next month."

"That's why the ATV couldn't come this way," Henry said.

"Right," said Kayla. "Even walking too close

to their nest could disturb them. The fence helps protect them. If the birds don't think it's safe here, they might leave."

Benny put his hand on the fence. "All of this is just for two birds? Why are they so important?"

"We have to protect all rare species, remember?" Henry said. "Big or small, cute or plain. They're all important."

"Oh, right." Benny peered between two boards. "Hi, little birds. Stay safe."

"That isn't all," Kayla said. "These birds also have a very important role on the beach. They are an indicator species."

Benny turned to her. "What's an indy—that thing you said?"

"An indicator species shows the health of the whole area," she explained. "If that species is doing well, the area is probably doing well too. If the species is struggling, you have a problem. If the species is gone, it shows a *big* problem."

"They're like an early warning signal," Henry said.

"If piping plovers are in trouble, the whole beach may be."

"Exactly," Kayla said. "That's why we watch these plovers carefully. We want them to survive. We also want to see what they tell us about all the other plants and animals here."

"Are piping plovers endangered?" Violet asked.

Kayla nodded. "Yes, and they almost went extinct. At one time, there were fewer than eight hundred pairs on the whole Atlantic coast. Finally people decided to protect them. Now there are more than two thousand pairs. See? Conservation can work—if we work at it."

"That's good." Violet pulled out her sketchbook. She wanted to remember these birds.

"Our work isn't done though," Kayla added. "The birds face the same dangers as before. Too many beaches and shorelines are getting developed with buildings, destroying their habitat. Also, pets like cats and dogs can attack the birds, and people can disturb the dunes. The fence helps our little friends stay safe."

One bird flew over the sand dunes. He called with a shrill, piping note.

"That's the male," Kayla said. "He's telling the female he'd like to be her mate."

The male bird landed a few feet away from the female. He crept closer. Once he was nearby, he stood upright with his neck stretched out. He raised his feet one at a time, kicking high.

Violet laughed. "He looks like he's marching."

The female moved away from him slowly. He followed.

Violet sketched some sand dunes behind the birds in her picture. Then she waved good-bye as the birds ran back among the dunes. Violet was happy the work Kayla was doing seemed to be helping the plovers. She hoped they would continue to stick around—not only for their sake, but for the whole beach's.

CHAPTER 3

A Perfect View

On the way back to town, the Aldens continued to explore. The area wasn't blocked off, so they went into the dunes. They found all kinds of plants growing right out of the sand. Kayla explained that the plants had slowly changed over many, many years to live there. They had adapted to the soil.

"Plants and animals need the right habitat," Kayla

said. "Some can only live in wet rain forests. Others only live in dry deserts. These plants and animals are perfect for this place."

"People are animals too," Jessie said.

"That's right," Kayla agreed. "People have adapted to live many places. That makes us special. We also like to change the places where we live. We build houses. We pave roads and parking lots. We have offices and huge stores. These changes help us stay comfortable, but they can also cause harm. The animals and plants living there might not like the changes. It might be harder for them to survive."

Benny smiled up at her. "That's why people like you try to help the animals. And me too someday!"

Kayla smiled back. "The animals will be happy to have your help."

In the dunes, Violet drew more pictures. Jessie made notes. Henry helped Benny climb up the steep slopes. Finally, they were tired and hungry. They emptied sand from their shoes and went back to town to meet Grandfather and Mr. Young at a restaurant for dinner.

When they were done eating, Benny patted his stomach. "I am full! Unless there's dessert. I still have room for dessert."

Grandfather laughed. "Maybe later. Before that, I have a surprise for you. But we need to hurry to get there in time."

The Aldens said good-bye to Kayla and her father and got into Grandfather's car.

"What's the surprise?" Benny asked as he buckled his seatbelt.

"If I told you, it wouldn't be a surprise," Grandfather said.

"It could be a phone call to Mrs. McGregor and Watch," Jessie said. She missed their housekeeper and their dog back in Greenfield.

Henry sat in the front seat. He turned back to look at his siblings. "Grandfather said we had to hurry. That means this thing happens at a certain time."

"Not calling Mrs. McGregor then," Jessie said.

They drove down the road that ran near the coast. Sometimes they could see the ocean. At other times, the sand dunes blocked the view.

"It could be a movie or a play," Violet said.

Henry shook his head. "A movie or play would be in town. We're going away from where people live."

They knew they would find out the surprise soon. Still, it was fun to try to solve this little mystery.

The sun dropped lower in the sky. It turned the sand dunes golden. Light sparkled on the ocean.

"Oh, look!" Henry said from the front passenger seat. "A lighthouse!"

The other children leaned forward to see better. "It looks pink," Violet said. "That's because the sun is low. I bet it's really white."

Grandfather turned off the main road. He drove down a short, winding road toward the lighthouse.

"Grandfather!" Jessie said. "Is the lighthouse our surprise?"

Grandfather pulled into a parking space. "That's right. We're going to watch the sunset from the top!"

The children piled out of the car. They looked up at the lighthouse a short distance away. It was so tall!

They would have a great view from the top.

A man walked toward them from the lighthouse and met them at a gate. He opened it and shook hands with Grandfather.

"Children, this is Robert Williams," Grandfather said. "He will be our tour guide." He introduced the four children.

Mr. Williams seemed to be about Grandfather's age. But he had dark circles under his brown eyes, which made him look even older.

"We'd best hurry if you want to see sunset," he said with a yawn. "We have to go up a lot of steps."

The children wanted to run ahead to the lighthouse, but they slowed down to keep pace with Mr. Williams and Grandfather. Mr. Williams opened the lighthouse door with a key. He put his hand over his mouth to cover another yawn. "Excuse me. I haven't been sleeping well."

Inside the lighthouse their footsteps echoed as they entered a round room. Stairs with a metal handrail led up and up and up in a spiral.

Benny stood in the center of the room. He turned in a circle as he looked up at the spiraling stairs. "I'm getting dizzy!"

Grandfather ruffled his hair. "Then stop turning in circles."

"I like getting dizzy," Benny said, spinning one more time.

Mr. Williams looked at his watch. "We should move along." He started up the steps, and the children got in line behind him.

A few steps up, Mr. Williams paused. His breathing was loud. He moved to the side. "Maybe you children should go on ahead. I thought I was in good shape before I started this job. I walked a couple of miles every day. Turns out that's different from all these steps."

"Should we go ahead?" Jessie asked Grandfather.

"Yes, just be careful and don't touch anything." Grandfather stayed behind with Mr. Williams as the children went on up. It was a lot of steps! Henry counted 217 of them.

Finally, they reached the top and entered a large room with glass walls.

Jessie pointed to a big glass structure in the center of the room. "That must be the light." It was taller than any of them! "I wouldn't want to be here when the light was on," she said. "It must be very bright."

They waited quietly until Mr. Williams and Grandfather joined them. When they arrived Mr. Williams took a minute to catch his breath.

"Let's see," Mr. Williams said once he was ready. "We're in the lantern room. The tower is brick, but as you see, this room is made of glass in metal frames. The panes must be kept clean so ships at sea can see the light at night."

Benny pointed. "I see a ship out there right now."

"More than one," Henry said. "They are really far away though."

Benny turned to Mr. Williams. "Will they come close? We could look down at a ship and wave to people!"

"They'd better not come close!" Mr. Williams

said. "Port Elizabeth is too small for that kind of traffic. Those ships go to bigger ports along the coast."

Jessie stood close to the glass and peered out. "One small boat is closer to us," she said. "It's that old-fashioned boat we saw earlier."

Mr. Williams looked out too. "Oh yes, that's Linda Tanaka's tugboat."

"Of course," Henry said. "We were wondering what it was. Tugboats help bigger boats move by pushing or pulling them, if I remember correctly."

Benny grinned at his big brother. "Like you help me by pushing me on the swings?"

"Something like that," Henry said. "Some of the big ships can't come to shore safely on their own. The tugboat pushes them to the dock."

"That's right," Mr. Williams said. "Around here, the really big ships can't dock at all. The water isn't deep enough, and they would damage the shoreline. The tugboat brings supplies to the big ships. They stay out in the ocean where it's deep. Linda has been running that tugboat for years." He paused to yawn again.

"Port Elizabeth is more of a fishing town," Grandfather said.

"We met a man in the fishing competition," Jessie said. "He was fishing for striped bass."

"Half the town is in that competition," Mr. Williams said. "They're out day and night trying to catch the biggest one."

"Are you in the fishing competition?" Henry asked. "Is that why you're so tired?"

"I'm tired because I'm up all night." Mr. Williams yawned. "But not because I'm fishing. I started this job last week, and I live in the lighthouse keeper's house down on the point. That light is so bright! I don't know if I can get used to living so close by."

"I guess you have to be nearby," Henry said. "If anything goes wrong, you need to fix it right away."

"Yes," Benny said. "Otherwise one of those big ships might crash." He smacked his hands together and made a crashing sound.

Mr. Williams leaned on the railing. "Fortunately, I don't have to worry about that. Big ships like that are run by electronics these days. Computers tell them exactly where they are. They can run in the dark or in a storm. Nothing slows them down."

"So you don't have to stay up all night?" Jessie asked. "You don't have to make sure the light is working?"

"Nope," he said. "It's all automatic these days. The light runs itself. I'll give my tours during the day. I'll sleep at night, if I can ever get used to the light, that is. Now, would you like to step out to the catwalk?"

Benny looked all around. "You have cats up here?"

Mr. Williams laughed. "The catwalk is the platform outside. It goes around this room. That's how they clean the windows."

Violet peered outside. "Is it dangerous?"

"The catwalk gets inspected every year." Mr. Williams opened a glass pane that was also a door. "It's sturdy. The railing will keep you safe. Just don't climb on it and don't run."

"We won't." Henry grabbed Benny's hand. Benny tried to follow the rules, but sometimes he got excited and forgot.

They went onto the catwalk and looked out. The lighthouse was on a narrow strip of land that came out from the mainland and turned north. In one direction they looked far out over the ocean. On the other side, they looked back toward the mainland. The sun was low on the western horizon. It turned the sky pink and glared off the glass of the lighthouse. Violet brought out her camera and took some pictures of the sunset. Then she took pictures of her family on the catwalk.

"The light will go on soon," Mr. Williams said. "You might not want to be here then. It's so bright!"

"Thank you for giving us a special tour," Grandfather said. The children added their thanks.

"Happy to do it. Soon I'll be giving tours every hour throughout the day. I need to start getting in shape now. If I keep this job, I'll be running up and down those stairs in no time." Mr. Williams yawned again. "I just have to figure out how to get some sleep!"

Jessie felt sorry for the lighthouse keeper. He didn't seem to enjoy his job much. "Why do they still keep

the light on all night?" she asked Mr. Williams. "You said the ships don't need it."

"Port Elizabeth likes its lighthouse," Mr. Williams said. "It's historical. Tourists like it too. I suppose it is pretty—from a distance. And most small boats aren't as advanced as the big ships. Sometimes the tugboat goes out at night. The lighthouse helps Linda see where she is."

Violet took Grandfather's hand. "This was a very good surprise."

He squeezed her hand. "I'm glad you like it. We still have to settle into our home for the week. It's not far from here. Plus, it's near the beach, so you might see sunrise as well, if you're up for it."

They headed back down the lighthouse stairs. Then they thanked Mr. Williams again and said good-bye.

Grandfather drove to Mr. Young's house, where Grandfather's friend greeted them with bowls of ice cream for dessert. It was the perfect ending to their first day. But everyone was tired. After dessert they headed straight to bed, with the girls sharing one room and the boys sharing another.

Violet drifted to sleep thinking of all they had seen. She wished she'd gotten to sketch the lighthouse. Photos were great, but she liked drawings even better. Photos captured what her eyes saw. Drawings captured what her heart felt.

Sometime later, Violet awoke. The only light came from the clock by her bed. It said 2:43. Wondering what had woken her, she slipped out of bed and felt her way to the window. Heavy curtains covered the windows. She pulled them back and looked out.

The moon must not be up tonight, Violet thought to herself. She could see the stars, but it was still very dark out. As she looked over the water, she wondered if people were out fishing on the shoreline. *Maybe I heard someone from the beach*, she thought.

Violet yawned and went back to bed. It wouldn't be until the next day that she found out what had actually woken her up in the night.

CHAPTER 4

Rude Awakening

In the morning, the children gathered in Mr. Young's kitchen.

"Where's Grandfather?" Violet asked. "Aren't we spending the day at the beach?"

Henry held up a piece of paper. "He left a note. It says he and Mr. Young are already down there and that we should join them."

"Before breakfast?" Benny rubbed his belly.

"Take a granola bar if you're hungry," Henry said with a frown. There was something strange about Grandfather leaving so early in the morning.

When the children were ready, they headed out the back steps of the house and down to the beach. "The note said to turn toward town." Henry turned right and started walking.

"Do you think this is another surprise?" Violet asked.

Henry shrugged. "I guess we'll find out."

Jessie tried to imitate Grandfather's voice. "It's not a surprise if I tell you!" They all giggled.

A few minutes later, they saw people gathered ahead on the beach. "There's Grandfather," Jessie said. He and Mr. Young walked over to meet them. They both had serious looks on their faces.

"What is everyone looking at?" Jessie asked. "Is it a whale?"

"I'm afraid it's nothing good," said Mr. Young. He took off his hat and ran his hand over his bald head.

"There's been an accident. A boat ran aground in the night."

"Oh no! Is everyone all right?" Violet asked.

Grandfather patted her shoulder. "No people were hurt. But unfortunately, it left a big mess behind. A lot of oil spilled into the water."

They walked closer to the group, where Kayla was standing. In the distance they could see a boat in the water. The Aldens recognized it as the tugboat they'd seen the day before. It leaned slightly to one side as waves lapped around it.

Benny wrinkled his nose at what smelled like rotten eggs. "You said it ran aground. It's not on the ground. It's still in the ocean."

"*Aground* means the boat is touching the ground under the water," Henry explained.

"A sandbar runs out under the water," Mr. Young said. "Linda should have stayed farther from shore. She has thirty years' experience. I don't know what happened this time."

They all gazed at the tugboat and the other

small boats around it. A line of orange tubes snaked through the water. They looked like long balloons tied end to end. The orange line made a circle around the boat. Inside the circle the water was unnaturally dark and shiny.

Kayla noticed the Aldens. She looked tired, with shadows under her eyes. "What a disaster," she said. "The good news is I think we have most of the fuel trapped."

"Why was the tugboat out in the night?" Jessie asked.

"One of the cargo ships called it out," Kayla said. "Linda was supposed to deliver fuel. That's not unusual. But she ran aground on the way, and hundreds of gallons of heavy, black fuel spilled into the water."

"What are those orange things floating in the water?" Jessie asked.

"Those are called booms," Kayla said. "Oil will float on the water's surface. That's bad because birds can land in the oil. It can get on marine animals like seals too. It can also wash onto shore. That will hurt the habitats along the coast."

"The booms must be filled with air," Henry said. "They float on the water and form a wall."

"That's right," Kayla said. "The booms keep the oil contained to one area so it doesn't spread."

Jessie made some notes in her notebook. "That's good. But then what happens? You can't leave the oil on the water forever."

"We start by containing it," Kayla said. "We still have to clean it up."

They all looked out at the dark water. The booms made a large circle around the oil.

"How do you clean it up?" Benny asked. "Do you swim out there with buckets? Can we help?"

Kayla smiled. "That would take a long time. We have three ways of cleaning oil spills. One way uses chemicals to break up the oil into smaller droplets so that the oil mixes with the water."

Violet frowned. "I thought you wanted to get the oil out of the water."

"Right," Kayla said. "That's the problem with the

chemical method. It gets the oil off the surface of the water, but the oil droplets sink. They can affect the fish and animals that live deeper down. Sometimes it's the only option. However, you can't use it near shore. The waves would bring the oil in to land, harming the animals and people here."

"What are the other methods?" Henry asked.

"If you can keep all the oil together, you can burn it," Kayla said.

Jessie gasped. "Isn't burning oil bad? Doesn't it pollute the air?"

Kayla nodded sadly. "Sometimes you only have bad choices. Burning oil isn't as bad as leaving the oil in the water. But you can't use the burning method near shore either."

"You must be planning to use the third way," Henry said.

"You got it," Kayla said. "We're going to skim the oil. We have most of the oil trapped inside the booms. Now a skimmer will pick it up."

"Why don't you always use a skimmer?" Jessie

asked. "It sounds best."

"It is my first choice, but they can't always use it," Kayla explained. "A skimmer only works when the oil slick is thick. The ocean must be fairly calm. They won't get all of the oil with the skimmer. Some of it will stay in the water no matter what we do. But at least the skimmer helps."

"Can *we* help?" Violet asked.

Kayla shook her head. "I think we've done everything we can for now. Linda did the right thing. She called in as soon as it happened. Sometimes people don't want to admit they made a mistake. They try to hide it. She told us right away so we could act. We got the equipment out and trapped most of the oil. Now, we're just waiting for the skimmers."

She sighed. "It's not a huge spill, but it is still a disaster. We don't know exactly what will happen yet." She looked sad.

Benny pulled out his last granola bar. "Are you hungry? Sometimes I feel bad when I'm hungry. Then eating makes me feel better."

Kayla looked up and smiled. "Thanks, Benny. I'm sorry for my bad mood. You shouldn't worry. Everything is under control, and you're right, a good breakfast is the way to start the day. I missed mine."

Benny held out his granola bar. "You can have this."

Grandfather chuckled. "Benny must really like you if he's willing to share his snacks."

"I have a better idea," Kayla said. "Let's go into town and get some real breakfast."

"That is a great idea!" Benny said.

The others agreed. After all, they couldn't help with the oil spill and should probably stay out of the way.

They walked toward town. "This is the way to build an appetite," Jessie said. "I hope we go someplace that has pancakes."

Benny ran near the water. He liked the way the wet sand felt. "I always have an appetite! I don't need to build one."

"Right," Grandfather chuckled. "Your appetite is built in."

Closer to town, the beach was flat and sandy. It

wasn't hilly like the area with the sand dunes. Some people walked along the water. Two children made a sandcastle.

The sound of an engine grew louder. It didn't sound like a regular car. It was the loud, high-pitched sound of an ATV. As the all-terrain vehicle bounced down the beach, the Aldens recognized the red-and-black helmet. Jenny Mitchell sped past them.

Mr. Young looked after her and shook his head. "People shouldn't drive that fast. It's too close to town."

"She's not very careful," Henry said.

Jessie nodded. "I'd be afraid of running over a small animal."

"Even if you didn't hurt an animal, you might scare them," Violet said.

"Maybe she's in a hurry because she's hungry," Benny said. "Like me!"

Grandfather ruffled Benny's hair. "Okay, let's hurry to breakfast."

They walked along the boardwalk past the docks. They came to the pier with the fishing tournament leaderboard. The board now had names written on it, and a group of fishermen gathered around.

Austin Green, the man the children had met the day before, stood next to the board wearing his bright orange life preserver. "That's right. I'm at the top!" he told the others. "Last night I caught the biggest striper so far. It is almost a record breaker for this contest."

The older man from the day before gave a snort. "It's not that close to last year's winner. Someone could still get a bigger fish."

Austin grinned. "I have a feeling you won't see many more fish coming in."

Kayla frowned. "He may be right," she told the Aldens. "The oil spill and cleanup are going to affect the contest. All the activity might scare away the fish. Plus I can't imagine lots of people will want to go fishing after this. I wish Austin were taking it more seriously."

"I agree," said Jessie. "It's a disaster. He shouldn't be gloating."

"Where did you catch that big fish anyway?" the

older man asked. "I didn't see you out this morning."

A few other people agreed. No one had seen Austin Green fishing on the shoreline the night before.

Austin laughed. "You don't expect me to give away my secrets, do you? I'm in the lead, and I'll stay that way."

The Aldens and their friends walked on. "Could he really have a secret fishing spot?" Henry asked.

Mr. Young stroked his chin. "Could be. People who fish are secretive. If they have a good spot, they don't like sharing it."

"That will be especially true with the contest," Kayla said. "But how many secret fishing spots can there be around here? Some of these people have been fishing the area for fifty or sixty years. They must know every inch of the shoreline."

"That's true," her father said. "Still, you have to think about the tides and wind and water temperature. The weather has an effect—even the moon cycle! All that can change where the fish go."

"Wow, fishing is complicated," Henry said.

"That's what makes it fun," Mr. Young said. "It's about the challenge. One year a spot might be great. The next year it might be terrible."

They paused outside a diner. A sign in the window advertised pancakes, waffles, eggs, and more.

"So I guess Austin Green *could* have a great secret fishing spot," Henry said.

"He could," Kayla agreed. "Now with the oil spill, he could win the contest. It doesn't seem fair to me, but I guess I don't care." She shrugged. "We have more important things to do."

"We do!" Benny pulled open the restaurant door. "Like eating breakfast!"

The Big Spill Rescue

CHAPTER 5

More to the Story

The group sat at a big table and ordered food. When they were done, the waitress put a cup of crayons down. The paper placemats had outlines of fish and crabs. Benny grabbed a green crayon and started coloring.

The fish reminded Violet of the spill and all of the animals at risk. "I can't believe an oil spill happened in Port Elizabeth," she said. She had seen news stories about big spills happening before, but she never thought she would see one.

"Sadly, while big oil spills are rare, smaller ones are much more common," said Kayla. "Some are caused by carelessness. Others happen when big ships flush out their fuel tanks without following the right processes."

"Does anyone know why this one happened?" asked Jessie. "Mr. Williams at the lighthouse knows that boat captain. He said she has been running the tugboat for years."

"That's a good question," Kayla shook her head. "From what I gathered on the beach, people are mostly focused on the cleanup. I don't know what Linda Tanaka said about the accident."

Henry remembered how the tugboat looked. "That boat is pretty old. The paint was so faded I could hardly read the name on the side. Maybe the boat was falling apart."

Kayla stirred her coffee. "Linda takes good care of her boat where it matters. She'd notice if something big was wrong. In any case, age wouldn't make the tugboat run aground. I guess maybe the engine could fail. Then waves and wind could push the boat onto the sandbar."

"She ran aground when the tide was going out," Mr. Young said. "The waves shouldn't have pushed her onto the sandbar."

"It's strange." Kayla sipped her coffee. "The shoreline is marked with buoys."

Benny looked up from his coloring. "I don't know about other *boys*, but I was in bed last night!"

Kayla giggled. "Buoys, Benny, not boys. Buoys are markers that sit above the water. It's strange though. Linda has lived here for decades. I'll bet she knows where she is just by the lighthouse."

Violet remembered Mr. Williams saying how the lighthouse was so bright he couldn't sleep at night. Suddenly, she sat up straight. She had remembered something.

"What is it?" asked Jessie.

Violet told them about the night before. Something had woken her up, but she hadn't figured out what. "It was just dark," Violet said. "At the time I didn't think anything of it."

"It's supposed to be dark at night," Benny said.

"It is," said Violet. "But not in Port Elizabeth…"

"Oh!" Jessie looked at her sister. "It's supposed to be bright because of the lighthouse."

Violet nodded. "The lighthouse wasn't on! I looked at the clock. The time was two forty-three."

"We put blackout curtains on those windows," Mr. Young said. "That keeps it dark inside at night. Even the lighthouse light can't get through those curtains."

"I looked out the window," Violet said. "I saw the stars."

"Are you sure?" Kayla asked. "I know Mr. Williams is new at his job. Still, the lighthouse should go on by itself. It runs automatically."

Violet nodded. She was sure.

The waitress came with their food, and everyone dug into plates of eggs, bacon, hash browns, and pancakes. The ate quietly while they considered Violet's news.

A few minutes later, Kayla looked up and waved. "Linda!"

A woman wearing a denim shirt and overalls with rubber boots entered the restaurant. She looked tired, with her hair uncombed and her eyes half closed. It was Linda Tanaka, the tugboat captain.

Mr. Young, who knew Linda well, invited her over. "Please join us," he said.

Linda sank down on a chair. "What a night. Worse than that big storm when we had all that rescue work. Worse for me, anyway."

"We were just talking about it," Kayla said. "Linda, I have a question. Was the lighthouse turned on last night?"

"I'm afraid not." Linda poured herself some coffee. She added cream and took a few sips. Finally she looked around at the rest of the group. "The light was working at first. Then around two thirty, it went out."

Linda shook her head. "I tried to turn on my floodlight, but it wouldn't go on. I found a replacement bulb, but that didn't help. I finally figured out a wire was loose. I must have gotten off course during all that running around."

"What happened when you finally got your floodlight on?" Henry asked.

"That light isn't nearly as bright as the lighthouse. I couldn't see shore. I was looking around for buoys. They show hazards like reefs and sandbars."

"I saw some of them this morning," Henry said. "One had a bird perched on it."

"Buoys, not boys," Benny said. "*I* don't want a bird on my head!"

Linda was too tired to know quite what Benny was talking about. But she continued anyway. "Right, so I was trying to find one so I'd know where I was. Before I spotted any, I ran onto the sandbar." She dabbed at her eyes with a napkin. "It's terrible. All that oil in the water. I've been doing this for thirty years without an accident. Now this!"

"Oh, Linda." Mr. Young patted her shoulder. "Accidents happen."

"You did the right thing after," Kayla said. "You got

help quickly. We'll be able to skim up most of the oil."

Linda sighed. "That's good, but it should never have spilled in the first place. I don't want any animals getting sick because of me."

The children looked at each other. They felt bad for Linda. She was clearly sorry for what happened.

"Last night sounds scary," Jessie said. "We're glad you're okay."

The other children nodded.

"Thank you." Linda finished her coffee and stood up. "I'm going to get some breakfast to go and head back down to the beach. I'm sure the authorities will want to talk to me again. They have to investigate this."

After she left, the Aldens and their friends finished their breakfast quietly. After such a great first day, the Aldens' trip had taken an unexpected turn. All they could think about was the big spill. Still, there didn't seem like much they could do.

When Jessie's plate was empty, she looked up. "We might not be able to help with the cleanup, but from what we've learned this morning, I think we might be able to help in another way."

"What do you mean?" asked Henry.

"The light in the lighthouse went out," said Jessie. "That was the cause of the oil spill. If we can figure out what went wrong, we can help make sure it doesn't happen again."

"You heard Linda," Kayla said. "The authorities will investigate."

Benny jumped up from his chair. "Yes, but we can investigate too. We are good at solving mysteries!"

Kayla smiled. "I've heard that about you. Is that really how you want to spend your vacation?"

"Of course," Jessie said. "I, for one, can't think about much else. It would be good to do what we can."

"Linda seemed nice," Violet said. "I don't want her to get in trouble if it's not her fault."

Henry and Benny agreed.

"All right." Kayla got up. "As long it's okay with your grandfather."

Grandfather nodded. "I know better than to stand

between my grandchildren and a mystery."

After breakfast Kayla showed the children where they could rent some bicycles for the day. They agreed to meet up with her at the beach later, to check in. Then they headed off to search for clues.

Their first stop was the lighthouse. As they rode up the hill and down the point, they were glad for their big breakfasts. Once they got near, they parked their bicycles by the lighthouse fence.

"Now we have to find Mr. Williams," said Jessie.

"Do you think he is in the lighthouse?" Violet asked.

Henry looked around the parking lot. "I don't see any cars. If there's no tour, he's probably not in the lighthouse. He said he lived in a house nearby."

Jessie pointed at a small cottage near the parking lot. "That must be it."

They walked down the path to the lighthouse keeper's house and knocked on the door. After a moment Mr. Williams appeared. "Good morning," he said with a smile. "Are you back for another tour?"

Henry was surprised at how cheerful he seemed.

"Actually, we wanted to ask you something," he said. "Do you know about the tugboat running aground last night?"

Mr. Williams's smile faded. "Yes, I'm afraid so. The authorities have already been here to check on why the lighthouse was not on. They decided it must be a malfunction."

"What's a mal...thingy?" Benny asked.

"That means the equipment didn't work as it should," Mr. Williams said. "It didn't function normally."

"That doesn't explain why it happened," Henry said. "Did you notice anything else strange?

Mr. Williams squinted as he thought. "Let's see. Like I told the authorities, I did wake up at one point. This was when the light was still on, but I couldn't figure out why I had woken up."

"That happened to me too," said Violet. "At first I thought it might have been a noise, but I think it was the light going out of the lighthouse."

"A noise, huh?" said Mr. Williams. "Now that you mention it, I do remember hearing something.

At the time, I didn't think much of it. But it sounded like an engine."

"Like a car?" Henry asked.

"No, it didn't quite sound like a car." Mr. Williams scratched his head. "I'm not sure. By the time I woke up fully, it had stopped. I looked out to see if anyone was at the gate. I didn't see anyone, so I went back to bed." His smiled returned. "After that I slept like a baby for once!"

The children thought about what he'd said. They were surprised that he seemed to be in such a good mood. "May we look around?" Henry asked Mr. Williams.

"Sure." Mr. Williams grabbed his hat. "I'll come too. I have energy today."

They checked the gate. "I don't think a vehicle could get through here," Henry said. "If one was here last night, it stopped in the parking lot."

"I would have seen a vehicle in the parking lot," Mr. Williams said.

"Wasn't it dark?" Jessie asked.

"It was still light then. I remember that much." Mr. Williams looked around. "The lighthouse doesn't shine directly down here. Still, it lights up the area pretty well. It flashes past my window every fifteen seconds."

"Maybe someone parked before they got to the parking lot," Henry said. "If they stayed on the road, we won't find tracks. Let's look around the lighthouse."

They walked around the outside of the lighthouse but didn't see anything strange.

"Where are the controls for the light?" Henry asked. "Are they all the way at the top?"

"No, they're here at the base. I'll show you." Mr. Williams unlocked the lighthouse door.

They all went into the first room. Mr. Williams pointed at a power box on the wall, and Henry pulled it open.

"The power was on this morning," Mr. Williams said. "It's on a timer. The timer was off by over three hours. Something stopped the electricity to the timer last night." He shrugged. "Everything works fine now. Just like the authorities said, it was a malfunction."

Henry was not so quick to jump to that conclusion. "What's this?" He pointed at some threads snagged on the corner of the power box.

Mr. Williams looked over Henry's shoulder. "I don't know. I've never noticed them there before."

"Do you ever wear anything this color?" Jessie asked. The threads looked to be a bright red or orange.

Mr. Williams laughed. "Orange is not really my color. Maybe when the officials checked the box, one of them caught a sleeve on there."

"Maybe..." Henry said. "Are you sure you locked up last night?"

"Of course." Mr. Williams hesitated. "I think so? I must have."

"Was it locked this morning?" Henry asked.

Mr. Williams thought for a minute. "You know, I assumed it was locked. I didn't check. I just put my key in the lock."

Jessie made notes in her notebook. "Mr. Williams, what time did you hear the noise and look out?"

"I believe it was a little after two," he answered.

Jessie wrote that down.

"Thank you for letting us look around," Henry said. "We'll let you know if we learn anything."

Mr. Williams headed back to his house, and the children went to their bikes.

"I think those threads were a clue," Violet said.

"I agree," Henry said.

Jessie looked over her notes. "Mr. Williams heard the engine and looked outside a little after two. He said the light was on at that time. Linda Tanaka said the light went out at around two thirty. Violet, you said it was dark at two forty-three."

"The times fit," Henry said. "Maybe someone came out at two a.m. They might have hidden from Mr. Williams if they heard his door open. Then they got into the lighthouse to turn off the light."

Jessie looked toward Mr. Williams's house. "He says he locked up, but he doesn't seem sure. Plus, he was very tired yesterday. Maybe he forgot."

"You mean the lighthouse was open all night?" Benny asked.

"It might have been," Henry said. "I think there's more to this story."

Jessie shivered. "So the tugboat accident might not have been an accident. Someone might have turned out the light on purpose."

"You know what this means?" Benny asked.

Henry grinned. "You're ready for lunch?"

Benny shook his head. "No. Well, maybe. But this means we have a real mystery!"

CHAPTER 6

Helping Hands

After visiting the lighthouse, the Aldens headed to the beach to meet up with Kayla. They dropped off their bicycles at a bike rack in the parking lot and then headed down to the sand, where Kayla stood with her hands on her hips. She was looking out over the water.

"They're using the skimmers now," Kayla said

once they joined her. She pointed toward a small boat floating inside the orange booms. Someone stood on the boat wearing a blue jumpsuit and an orange life jacket. He held a long tube about six inches wide. The tube went from a machine on the boat into the water. The sound of a motor rumbled across the water.

"The skimmer sucks up the oil from the water's surface," Kayla said. "It's like a vacuum cleaner."

"Where does the oil go?" Benny asked.

"Into a storage tank in the boat," Kayla said. "Later they will empty the tank and clean the oil. The clean oil can then be used again."

"Neat!" Benny said.

Jessie pulled out her notebook. "So the booms keep the oil in one place. The skimmers clean it up." She jotted notes.

Kayla nodded. She was impressed with how interested the Aldens were in the cleanup. "We're lucky the sea is fairly calm. Skimming doesn't work well when the water is choppy. Even the small waves today will carry some oil over the booms. The tide is coming in now. That means more oil will wash to shore."

She crouched in the sand at the water's edge. "Watch when the waves go out. See how the sand is black and shiny? That's oil that washed to shore."

Violet wrinkled her nose. "Yuck. I wouldn't want to walk on that sand or swim here."

Kayla stood up. "No. But fish and animals don't always have a choice. Animals like clams burrow under the sand. That keeps them away from the oil. However, they may eat polluted food. That's not good for them."

"The oil makes for an unhealthy beach," said Jessie. "I wish we could do something to help."

"I have good news about that," said Kayla. "Because of the size and urgency of the cleanup, they are accepting volunteers. They've agreed to let us help!"

"Us?" Henry asked. "Do you mean Protectors of Animals Worldwide?"

"Yes. And my very helpful assistants." Kayla gave them a wink. "If you'd like, that is."

The children shouted their agreement. Then they went and got their bikes and rode them into town, where the cleanup was happening. Inside a school gym, PAW had set up long tables. Each of the Aldens would help a member of PAW. Jessie was paired with Kayla.

"Animal control is bringing in birds and other animals." Kayla pointed at a man carrying a large plastic tub. "You need experts for that kind of thing. Wild animals are hard to catch. You might hurt them more if they fight to get away."

Jessie remembered an article she'd read. After an oil spill, people washed the affected animals. "Are we going to wash them?"

Kayla nodded. "But only after the vets say it's okay. Getting a bath is stressful to a wild animal. They have to be healthy."

Jessie and Kayla paused by a table where several veterinarians were examining animals. They listened to the animals' breathing. They counted the heartbeats.

"Some animals may need fluids or food," Kayla

said. "Others may be sick or injured. The vets will treat them. Once they are healthy, we can wash them."

"I understand," Jessie said. "Are some animals ready now?"

"Yes. During a bigger spill, animals may spend days covered in oil. They can't fly or swim, so they can't catch food. They get thin and sick. Those animals need rest and food before they're washed. But we got to these animals a few hours after the spill. Most are in good health, except for the oil."

Kayla led the way to another table. She spoke to a woman at a computer who was tracking the animals as they moved through the system. A minute later Kayla picked up a plastic tub and moved it to a table where they had room to stand.

Kayla slowly opened the lid. Jessie peeked inside and saw a bird that was about a foot long. Its thin, pointy beak was black. It had orange legs. The feathers on its neck and breast stuck together. They were covered with dark, shiny oil.

"This is a roseate tern," Kayla said. "It's an

endangered species, and right now is it's breeding season. We'll want to get her back out as quickly as possible. Otherwise she might not nest."

Kayla and Jessie put on white jumpsuits to protect themselves from the nasty oil. Kayla gently lifted the bird into a tub of warm water. "This is clean water with a little dishwashing liquid."

"You mean you wash birds just like you would wash dishes?" Jessie asked.

"I suppose so," Kayla said, spreading soap bubbles over the bird, "that is, if you're very gentle with your dishes. We don't want to use harsh chemicals. Research shows that dish soap removes most oils. It doesn't irritate the animals' skin or eyes, and it rinses out quickly from feathers. Sometimes a simple answer is best."

"Why is this bird endangered?" Jessie asked. "People don't hunt them, do they?"

"Not anymore," Kayla said. "Years ago, people killed the birds for their feathers. They used the feathers in hats. But now the birds are protected."

"That's good!" Jessie couldn't imagine why someone would kill a bird for hat feathers.

"They're still in trouble." Kayla stroked the bird's back. "Roseate terns are easily disturbed. If they sense a threat, they'll leave their nest. That's why we close off nesting areas. We don't want people or dogs to scare the animals."

Jessie thought about their dog, Watch. He wouldn't kill a bird, but he might chase one. Watch thought that was fun, but the birds might not know it was a game.

"Cats kill a lot of birds as well," Kayla said. "House cats should never go outside unless someone is watching them."

"A pet cat doesn't need to catch its food," Jessie said.

"No, but some of them still like to hunt. It's an instinct. Owners don't always realize. They think their cat likes to go outside to explore. Really the cat is killing birds or rodents every day. Loss of habitat is a problem, too, as people build houses or hotels near the beaches. Now sea levels are rising due to climate change as well. That takes away more places where animals live."

Jessie sighed. "It's all so much."

Kayla put her arm around Jessie. "I know. But we can help this bird. We can help lots of animals today. And we can make changes to help the planet and all the animals on it. We have to do what we can."

"Right!" Jessie gave a firm nod. "Let's help this bird. What should I do?"

"We'll move her to the next tub now. She'll get several washes in clean, soapy water." Kayla showed Jessie how to wash the bird. Jessie took her turn. She felt the bird's heart beating rapidly in its chest.

Slowly, the dark oil came out of its feathers. As the bird got clean, they could see its colors better. It had a white body with gray wings and a black cap.

Jessie and Kayla used several tubs of water. They didn't stop until the bird was all clean. Then they took the tern to the rinsing area, where they used a hose with a spray nozzle. Jessie held the bird's body with one hand and gently stretched out its wing with her other. It was strange to be touching a wild bird.

"We need to get all the soap out," Kayla said, spraying the top of the wing. "Otherwise the bird won't be waterproof. She might sink instead of float! She won't be able to stay warm with wet feathers either."

Finally they took the bird to the drying area. This area held special cages for the animals. Dryers used for grooming pets blew warm air into the cages. The tern squirmed and ruffled its feathers.

"Here our friend will use her beak to preen," Kayla said. "Preening is when a bird cleans and straightens its feathers. All the feathers have to be smooth. They'll overlap to make a waterproof seal."

Jessie crouched by the pen, watching the tern. "How long does that take?"

"The whole process takes several days," Kayla said. "Once the bird is dry, she'll go to a warm pool. She will keep preening and bathing. We'll make sure she can float and swim."

"You'll feed her, right?" Jessie asked.

"Absolutely! We'll make sure she gets everything she needs. The veterinarians will check on all the animals. We'll release her once we know she's healthy. She must be able to swim, preen, and feed on her own."

Jessie stood. "I didn't know cleaning a bird took so long. It's a lot different from bathing our dog, Watch."

"You probably don't need a whole team for your dog." Kayla gestured around the room. At least thirty people were at work.

"Well, sometimes it does take all four of us." Jessie looked down at her wet jumpsuit. "And we wind up just as wet! Will this tern be okay?"

"Her chances look good," Kayla said. "You did a great job helping."

Jessie smiled. "Let's wash another one."

By dinnertime everyone was tired but happy. All the Aldens had enjoyed helping animals. Violet had helped wash an angry seagull. They'd had to put a towel over the bird's head to keep it calm. Henry had worked with a group taking water samples. They wanted to see how far the oil had spread. He got to see a humpback whale out in the ocean. Benny helped clean animals, too, and finished the day soaked from head to toe. He loved every minute of it.

"It sounds like you all did a great job," Grandfather said. "I know it's hard seeing animals in trouble."

Henry nodded. "I liked seeing all the people helping. That made me feel good."

"I got so dirty and wet," Violet said. "But it was worth it!"

"I talked to the animal doctors!" Benny said. "They know everything."

Grandfather chuckled. "They do know a lot. Let's take a break and celebrate tonight. I planned something special."

Violet sat up straighter. "Ooh, another surprise? What is it?"

Grandfather smiled. "Remember? It wouldn't be a surprise if I told you."

After dinner they all piled in the car, and Grandfather drove up the coastline away from Port Elizabeth. Before long they passed a sign for a national park and pulled into a parking lot. A tour guide met them and introduced himself as Philip Lucero. "Tonight we'll be touring the sand dunes," he said. "Then we'll have a bonfire on the beach."

He led the way among the sand dunes, which were much bigger than the ones the Aldens had seen before. Philip talked about all the plants and animals. So many things lived in this one area. Jessie scribbled notes. Violet took photos.

"We saw a woman on an ATV," Benny said. "That looked fun. She wanted to drive through the dunes. Can people do that here?"

"No," Philip said. "People can only ride ATVs where they are allowed. Not here. ATVs cut through the soil surface. This causes erosion—the loose sand blows away. To preserve the sand dunes, we need to keep vehicles away."

They came to the top of a dune. They could see up and down the coast and out over the water. Flowers made splashes of color among the grasses. Birds darted past, hunting bugs.

"Isn't it beautiful?" Philip stretched out his arms. "We wouldn't want to lose this."

"Could we really lose it?" Benny asked. "Where would it go? It's so big!"

Philip nodded. "We could lose it all if we don't take care of it."

"Remember how Kayla said everything is connected?" Jessie asked Benny.

"That's right," Philip said. "The soil and the plants. The animals and birds and insects. The ocean, too, and lakes and rivers, and even rain clouds. If you disturb one, you can hurt the others."

"I see," said Henry. "If the soil erodes, the plants won't grow as well."

"And then the bugs and insects won't be around," said Jessie.

"Or the things that eat them," said Violet. "Like the piping plover."

Philip nodded again. He was impressed with how much the Aldens had learned. "That's right. And that's why when you see birds like the piping plover, you know the habitat is doing well. The soil, the plants, the insects, and the bugs."

After touring the dunes and enjoying the scenery, the Aldens ended up on the beach. Large logs were arranged in a circle. In the center, rocks made a fire pit. Philip told them that fires weren't allowed everywhere on the beach, but they were allowed for the tours.

Henry helped stack the wood. Benny helped put marshmallows on sticks for s'mores.

As the fire started burning, the sun set, turning the sky pink. Jessie yawned. "I'm tired, but this was a good day. I got to touch a wild bird! And I learned so much."

"Me too," Violet said. "I'm sorry about the oil spill, but I'm glad we could help."

Henry was quiet for a moment. Then he spoke up. "I still want to know why it happened," he said. "We got so busy this afternoon that we didn't even get to think about the mystery at the lighthouse."

"We will," Benny said. "We'll help, just like we helped the animals today."

CHAPTER 7

A Clue in the Sand

In the morning, the Aldens gathered around the breakfast table at the Young house with Grandfather, Mr. Young, and Kayla. Mr. Young pulled a casserole dish out of the oven. "Baked French toast! I hope you're hungry."

"Yum!" Benny rubbed his tummy. "I hope you made two of those. I could eat one all by myself."

Mr. Young laughed. "We also have plenty of fruit. How about one serving of baked French toast and all the fruit you can eat?"

Benny agreed, and they all dug into their breakfasts.

"Are we going to wash more animals today?" Jessie asked Kayla.

"Animal control will keep looking for animals that need help," Kayla said. "We got most of the animals cleaned up yesterday. A few need more time to recover before they can be washed, but they have enough helpers now. The town really came out to help!"

"That's too bad," Violet said. "I mean it's too bad we can't help again! It's good that most of the animals are okay and that lots of people are helping."

"I have another job you can do," Kayla said. "We need volunteers to pick up debris that has washed ashore."

"Are debris some kind of fish?" Benny asked.

"No, debris means small pieces of garbage," Kayla said. "If something gets destroyed, the bits left behind are debris. We'll look for pieces of the tugboat that broke off and washed to shore. We might also find small balls of tar. The oil that washed onto the sand will start clumping together. Once it makes big enough clumps, we can pick it up. Of course, you might find other garbage too. It should all be cleaned up."

"We'd be glad to help," Henry said. The other children agreed.

They finished breakfast and headed to the beach, where a group of volunteers had gathered. One man wore thin rubber gloves and held something that looked to be moving. A woman knelt in the sand next to him, digging through a supply bag.

Jessie stretched her neck trying to see what the man was holding. Then she covered her mouth. "Is that a turtle?"

"Oh my," said Kayla. She waved at the woman kneeling in the sand. "Hi, Lucia. I'd hoped it was too early for sea turtles to come ashore."

The young woman looked up. She had short black hair with purple streaks and wore a PAW T-shirt. "This little guy is early. He had bad timing.

Now he's covered in tar."

The man was holding the turtle with one hand. With the other, he was scrubbing away sticky black tar with a toothbrush.

"Can you save it?" asked Violet.

"We're certainly going to try," said Lucia. She pulled out a plastic syringe from the bag and stood up.

"Are you going to give the turtle a shot?" Benny asked.

"No, I'm going to give him mayonnaise." Lucia stuck the syringe into a jar and pulled the plunger to fill it. Then she gently turned the turtle's head toward her. She stuck her finger in the corner of its mouth and put the syringe in.

"Is that really mayonnaise?" Jessie asked. Turtles wouldn't eat mayonnaise in the wild.

"Yep." The man slowly pushed the plunger on the syringe. "The mayonnaise will help break down the tar. Then the turtle will be able to expel the tar."

"He means the turtle will poop out the tar," Kayla explained.

"I like mayonnaise on a sandwich," Benny said. "But it doesn't make me poop."

Kayla laughed. "Mayo is an emulsion. That's a mix of two things that don't usually mix well. Oil and water don't combine well."

"We remember," Henry said. "That's why the oil spill floated on top of the ocean."

"That's right," said Kayla. "Do you know how to make mayonnaise?"

"We don't make mayonnaise," Benny said. "It comes out of a jar."

Kayla smiled. "Someone has to make it," she said. "It's made of oil, egg yolk, and an acid like lemon juice. Egg yolk is the emulsifier. It binds the ingredients together. That way they won't separate. Otherwise you'd have yucky lumps. The emulsifier keeps the mix smooth."

Jessie frowned as she scribbled notes. "What does this have to do with turtles?"

"The emulsifier helps with the oil," Lucia said. "We can clean the outside of the turtle with soapy water. But what about the inside? We can't wash inside the turtle's throat. We can't wash its stomach. We need to break up the oil somehow. We feed the turtle mayonnaise to help break down the oil. Then it won't stick inside the digestive system."

"Wait a minute," Henry said. "I thought an emulsifier held things together."

"It's a little complicated," Kayla said. "The egg yolk helps the oil mix with the water. That way the oil doesn't clump up in the turtle's stomach. The egg yolk helps the oil move through the turtle's system."

"And come out as poop!" Benny said.

"The main thing to know is that the mayo can help." Lucia stroked the turtle's shell. "It will take a couple of weeks, but I think we saved this little one. We'll release it when it's healthy and the oil spill is gone. I hope we don't find any more turtles this week."

Kayla turned to the children. "If you see any turtles on the beach, don't touch them. Tell me right away, and we'll get them help."

"It's against the law to bother sea turtles," Violet said. "I saw a sign."

"That's right," Kayla said. "They are endangered, like so many animals. We have a phone number people can call if they see a turtle in trouble. The rest of the time, we leave them alone. Now, shall we get to work?"

Watching the turtle rescue was interesting, but the children couldn't help with that. They could do more good cleaning up debris. Kayla passed out garbage bags. She also gave each person thin rubber gloves. That way they wouldn't have to touch garbage. If they picked up balls of oil, it wouldn't stick to their hands.

"You get started," Kayla said. "I'll follow after I get the other volunteers going."

The group spread out and walked up the beach. Henry walked at the edge of the water. The waves lapped over his shoes. The other children spread out in a line up the beach.

Henry bent to pick up a piece of plastic. "We need to get back to the mystery," he said. "What made the lighthouse go out that night?"

"I think Mr. Williams is a suspect," said Benny. "I know how grumpy I get when I can't sleep. What if he turned out the light himself?"

"Maybe," said Violet. She had to admit that Mr. Williams had a clear reason to turn out the lighthouse. Still, she didn't want to believe it was him.

"We can't rule him out," said Jessie. "But let's assume he's telling the truth for a moment. He said he heard a sound. Maybe some kind of engine."

"We didn't find any vehicle tracks," said Violet. "Maybe the person parked before getting to the parking lot. But would Mr. Williams have heard the engine from there? That's pretty far from his house."

Henry thought back to the scene. "There are sand dunes between the road and his house. They would block sound. I don't think he would have heard an engine from the road. Besides, cars must drive past all the time. Why would he notice this time?"

"Then where did the car, or whatever it was, come from?" Jessie asked.

"Maybe it wasn't a car." Benny ran toward something that looked like garbage. When he picked it up, he saw it was only seaweed. "Maybe it was a plane that flew in!"

Jessie put a plastic straw in her garbage bag. "Sorry, Benny, I don't think a plane flew down to the lighthouse. Mr. Williams would definitely have noticed that!"

"Maybe a drone?" Henry said. "Someone could fly a drone with a remote control. Then again a drone couldn't open the lighthouse door. It couldn't turn out the lights. Someone had to go inside the lighthouse." He almost had another idea. He needed a moment to think.

Before he could say anything, Violet ran forward. "Look! Isn't this the piping plover area?" she called. "It is. I remember drawing those sand dunes. But where's the sign?"

The children gathered by the dunes.

"There it is." Jessie pointed at the sign, which was tipped over in the sand.

Henry hauled it upright. "Maybe the wind knocked it over." He pushed the bottom of the sign into the sand. Then he leaned on it hard and twisted to get the post into the sand. "This will have to do for now. We'll tell Kayla the sign should be fixed."

"I hope no one bothered the birds," Jessie said.

They watched the sand dunes where the nesting area was fenced off. This time no little birds ran past. The children didn't hear the piping sound the plovers made.

"Oh no," Violet said. "I'm afraid someone did scare the birds. Maybe they knocked down the sign on purpose. We need to tell Kayla."

Henry examined the area. He pointed to the sand. "It looks like there are tire tracks leading up into the dunes."

They walked over to the tire tracks and studied them. "Someone was driving where they shouldn't be." Henry crouched to look at the tracks. "They don't look like regular tracks. The tires that made these are wide. Look how deep these grooves are in the sand. The tires have a very deep tread."

"Who was the woman with the ATV?" Jessie snapped her fingers. "Jenny Mitchell. She didn't like hearing she couldn't drive here."

"She said she would have to find another way to make her riding more interesting," said Violet. "Even driving at night."

Henry stood and looked in the direction the tracks went. "They go toward the lighthouse." He turned to the others. "It looks like Jenny Mitchell was here. Could she have something to do with the lighthouse?"

Violet took a picture of the tracks. They could compare them to the ATV wheels. "Let's go tell Kayla," she said when she was done.

"Yes," Jessie said. "We need to find out what Jenny did and why."

CHAPTER 8

Off-Roading

When the children spotted Kayla coming down the beach, they waved to her excitedly, and she hurried over. Henry quickly explained about the tipped–over sign and the missing piping plovers.

Kayla sighed. "I'm not surprised. Remember, they are an indicator species. If they are here, that's a good sign. It means the environment is doing okay."

"The birds aren't here," Henry said. "That means the opposite."

Kayla nodded. "Think of what happened this week. The beach habitat is definitely not healthy."

Benny took Kayla's arm. "We have to tell you the rest. The lighthouse man said he heard a noise before the lighthouse went out. And look what we found!" Benny led her to the tire tracks.

Kayla knelt in the sand to study the tracks.

"Mr. Williams thought he heard an engine," Henry explained. "We didn't notice any ATV tracks around the lighthouse. But these tracks head in that direction."

"We are thinking the woman with the ATV might have something to do with the lighthouse going out," said Violet.

Kayla straightened and brushed sand off her knees. "An ATV could definitely make it down the point to the lighthouse. Did Mr. Williams tell you anything more?"

"He said he didn't think he heard a car engine," said Benny. "It was louder. It sounded like—" He broke off and turned toward the beach. "It sounded like that!"

Everyone turned to see an ATV headed up the beach. "It's red and black," said Jessie. "It must be Jenny again."

The ATV wove up and down the beach. Each time it turned, sand sprayed everywhere. Kayla waved her arms. Did Jenny see them? She had a helmet on. She might drive right past without spotting them.

Henry ran down the beach. He got in Jenny's path and waved his arms and yelled. He got ready to run out of the way if she didn't see him.

She kept coming toward him. Did she see him? How could she not?

Finally she slowed down and came to a stop a few feet away. She took off her helmet and shook out her hair. "You again?" She looked at Kayla and the other children as they ran down. "What's up?" Jenny asked.

Kayla crossed her arms and glared. "You are in big trouble!"

"Me?" Jenny pointed at herself. "What did I do? I turned back when you told me to the other day."

Henry spoke loudly over the noise of the engine. "You said you wanted to drive on the sand dunes, and we now know that someone did just that. They went past the sign for the restricted area."

"Well, it wasn't me," Jenny said.

"Are you sure?" Henry walked closer to the ATV. He studied the tire treads. "The tracks in the sand look just like your tire treads."

Jenny turned off the ATV. "Show me these tracks."

They marched to the sign by the piping plover area. Henry pointed to the tracks. "We can compare them to your tire tracks."

Violet pulled out her camera with a picture of the tracks.

Jenny frowned. "There's no need for that. You're right. These are mine. I drove down the beach the other night. I didn't go past any signs, I promise. When I realized I had gone too far, I turned back. I still don't see why it's so bad to ride in the sand dunes, but I didn't want to get into trouble."

"We have to protect the birds," Violet said.

"What's so great about this spot?" Jenny waved an arm toward the beach. Several seagulls ran through the wet sand. "There are birds all over the place. They're fine."

"These birds are special," Benny said. "They are in danger."

"They're endangered," Jessie explained. "They're called piping plovers."

Benny nodded. "The sand dunes are important. Animals live here that don't live anywhere else. When the sand dunes are hurt, the whole beach is hurt."

Jenny studied the dunes. "Really? I just see sand and weeds."

"Benny is right," Kayla said. "The sand dunes are a special habitat. The piping plovers are endangered, and a lot of their habitat has been destroyed. We need to protect the habitat they still have. If we don't, they could go extinct."

Benny looked up at Jenny. "I know you want to ride your ATV. It looks fun. But can't you ride it some-place else? Let the little birds have their sand dunes.

They need to nest so they can make more little birds."

Jenny smiled at Benny. "Thank you for explaining this to me," she said. "I'm used to people telling me no. They don't usually explain why. I thought they just wanted to spoil my fun. I don't want to cause any harm, so I'll stay away from this area."

"I'm glad you understand," Kayla said. "I hope it's not too late. If we keep people away from the sand dunes, maybe the plovers will come back. Maybe they can still nest this season."

Jenny went over to the sign. "I honestly didn't see this last night. I was looking for signs, but I must have missed it."

"It was on the ground," Kayla said. "You didn't knock it down on purpose?"

"No, I promise! Please, believe me." Jenny looked around at all of them.

"Her tire tracks don't go near the sign," Henry said.

"Well, maybe the wind blew the sign over," Kayla said. "Okay. I won't report you for riding in a restricted area."

"What about the lighthouse?" Violet whispered to Henry.

"Jenny, did you go to the lighthouse that night?" Henry asked.

Jenny shook her head. "When I saw the lighthouse, I stopped. That was when I realized I'd gone farther than I'd meant to. I turned back as soon as I saw it. Why?"

Henry explained about the light going out and the oil spill.

"That's terrible!" Jenny said. "I might not know about your endangered birds. But even I know an oil spill is bad. The light was on when I saw it. That was before midnight."

The children looked at each other. Jenny had admitted to driving where she shouldn't. She'd apologized. She seemed to feel bad about the lighthouse. They decided to let her go.

Jenny said good-bye and went back to her ATV. She turned around and drove down the beach. She didn't go as fast this time.

"I think she was telling the truth," Jessie said.

"She's not mean. She just didn't understand."

"I agree." Kayla tapped her finger to her lips. "So did someone turn out the light on purpose? If so, who did it?"

Henry frowned. "Someone did, but it wasn't Jenny on an ATV."

"So how did our mystery person get there?" Violet asked.

Henry's frown turned to a smile. "I have an idea."

CHAPTER 9

A Blue Clue

Kayla and the Alden children headed back to the lighthouse. Henry wanted to look for more clues to support his new idea. They spotted Mr. Williams holding a plastic trash bag. He waved and walked over to meet them.

"Hello, children! Hello, Kayla," he said, holding up his trash bag. "I'm picking up some debris the wind blew in. It's such a beautiful day to be outside."

Mr. Williams moved quickly, and he didn't have bags under his eyes like he had before. "You don't look tired anymore," Jessie said.

He beamed at them. "That is because I got some of those blackout curtains. They do a great job of keeping out the light. I woke up once last night and peeked out. I wanted to make sure the lighthouse was working. But the rest of the time, I slept like a baby."

"That's great," Jessie said. "I guess you'll like working here more now."

"I can't wait for tourist season." Mr. Williams laughed. "I'll get in great shape going up and down those steps ten times a day. Did you children want to go inside again?"

Henry was happy that Mr. Williams was not so tired. Still, he couldn't rule him out as a suspect just yet. Before Henry could decide what to believe, he needed to check some evidence.

"Actually," Henry said, "we wanted to go down to

the shore. We need to know why the light went out that night. We want to look for more clues."

"I'll join you," Mr. Williams said.

The group walked down a path toward the water. The path went through grass rather than sand dunes or sandy beach. It ended at an area of big rocks. They had to walk carefully on the rocks. As they got closer to the water, small waves splashed up. Water shot up in one area and then another, like a splash pad at a park.

The tide was going out, exposing more of the rocky shoreline. The rocks were wet and slippery with seaweed and algae.

"What are we looking for?" Mr. Williams asked.

Henry scrambled down a little closer to the water. "We don't think anyone came in a car or on an ATV. Benny suggested someone got here by air, but where would they land? One thing we haven't looked for is a boat."

"A boat makes sense," Kayla said. "But they're long gone. How will you prove a boat was here? How will you know which boat it was?"

"I have an idea," Henry said. "But we need one more clue."

"Try over there." Mr. Williams pointed to the left. "That's where I'd bring in a boat. You can get between the rocks if you're careful. There's even an iron ring someone pounded into a rock years ago. You could tie up a boat there."

The children carefully crept over the rocks. At times they had to crouch down and hold onto rocks with their hands. If they fell they might hurt themselves, and they would definitely get wet.

"I see the ring," Jessie said.

"Look, blue paint!" Violet grabbed a rock for balance. "It's on those pointy rocks to the right of the ring."

"Wait here." Henry made his way to the rock with blue streaks on it. He lay on his stomach and reached down to touch the blue area. A paint flake came off on his fingers. "Something scraped across here," he said. "Something painted blue. It must have been a boat, and it had to be recent. Otherwise, this would have washed away."

He got up. He put the paint flake in a clean tissue and put it in his pocket. Then he joined the others as they scrambled back to solid ground.

"So what does it mean?" Mr. Williams asked.

Henry no longer suspected Mr. Williams of turning out the lighthouse, so he told everyone what he was thinking. "Jenny wanted to drive her ATV on the sand dunes," Henry said. "But why would she drive all the way through the dunes to sabotage the lighthouse?"

"I don't think she would do that," said Jessie.

"So you think someone came in a blue boat, but who was it?" Kayla asked. "And why did they turn off the lighthouse? Surely no one would want to cause an oil spill."

"No," said Henry. "I think the person who sabotaged the lighthouse did it for another reason. They wanted to be out on the water without being seen."

"Who would do that?" asked Violet.

Jessie snapped her fingers. "Someone in the fishing competition! Boats aren't supposed to be allowed, but someone could have used one to get an advantage. Those fishermen said the best fishing happens at night."

"That makes sense," said Kayla. "The person wanted to cheat without getting caught. But who would do such a thing?"

"The same person who wears a life jacket that is the color of the orange threads we found in the lighthouse," said Henry.

"Can I see the paint?" Violet asked. Henry handed it over and she studied it. "I think you're right, Henry. It's navy blue, the same color as Austin Green's boat."

"The light went out during the night," Henry said. "And the next morning, Austin had the biggest fish. No one saw him fishing on the shoreline because he was out on his boat!"

"All that for a fish?" Kayla asked. She looked concerned but wasn't convinced yet. "Let's go talk with him."

They said good-bye to Mr. Williams and headed back to town. Because of the oil spill, no one was out fishing. All of the fishing boats were docked. Some people were using the time to work on their boats. One woman was painting the cabin of her boat a cheerful yellow. A man was scrubbing his deck.

The group paused on the pier to look at the scoreboard. It still showed Austin's name at the top. He would win the contest—unless they showed he had cheated. A man sat at a table next to the scoreboard. He was one of the official judges. "I think you should come with us," Kayla said.

Violet looked at the rows of boats. "There's Austin's. It's the third one on the right. See? It's the same navy blue as the paint on the rocks."

They walked down the pier, where Austin was dozing in a deck chair on his boat. He wore his usual flat-brimmed hat and orange life jacket.

"Ahoy, Austin!" Kayla called.

He sat up. "Hello." He looked at Kayla's frown. He looked at the official. Then he gave a weak smile. "Is…is everything okay?"

"You—you—" Kayla was so mad she could hardly speak.

Henry took over. "You turned off the lighthouse two nights ago."

Austin's mouth dropped open. "What? How do you—I mean—what do you mean?"

"We found orange thread caught in the power box." Henry pointed to Austin's life jacket. "Orange like that. We also found blue paint on the rocks at the edge of the water." He pulled out the tissue and showed the paint flake. "It's the same color as your boat."

Jessie crouched to look at the side of Austin's boat. "I can see where the paint got scraped off!"

"You went out at night to fish," Henry said. "You didn't want anyone to see you, so you turned the lighthouse's light off to keep it dark."

Austin slumped back in his chair. He put his hands over his face and let out a long sigh.

Then he dropped his hands and stood. "You're right. I wanted to win the fishing tournament so badly. I wanted to prove how good I am. I know a great spot where the biggest stripers come in. I just

needed to find a way to get there without being seen."

The official frowned and shook his head. "I'm afraid your biggest fish doesn't count. In fact, you're out of the tournament. You're disqualified for cheating."

Austin groaned. "I've been waiting for this for two days. I've been worried sick someone would find out."

"Well, everyone will," the official said. "I'm going to erase your name from the board right now!"

Other fishermen gathered around. They marched down to the scoreboard to erase Austin's name.

Austin watched them go. "I wanted to be the best," he said. "I couldn't think of anything except winning. What a terrible mistake I made! Now everyone knows I cheated."

"It's worse than that," Kayla said. "Your actions caused a lot of damage. Animals were hurt by the oil spill. It will affect the shoreline for months, and it's costing a lot to clean up."

Austin winced. "I'm sorry. I only meant to have the light out for a little while. I didn't think anyone would notice! I hadn't even thought of the tugboat being called out."

"You shouldn't have cheated," Jessie said. "If you hadn't, this accident would not have happened."

All the children nodded.

"What you did was criminal," Kayla said. "Maybe you didn't mean to cause the spill. But your actions had serious effects, and you will have to face the consequences."

"All right. I deserve it." Austin stepped down to the pier. "What do I have to do now?"

"We'll go talk with the authorities," Kayla's said. "You can turn yourself in. You'll probably get a big fine. You might need to do community service work. I don't think you'll go to jail though."

"I'll do what I can to fix things," Austin said. "I wanted to volunteer with the cleanup. I was afraid, though. I didn't want anyone asking questions, so I stayed away."

They walked down the pier. The men and women from the fishing contest were gathered around the scoreboard. Austin Green's name was gone. People congratulated the woman who was now on top. They hardly noticed Austin leaving in disgrace.

"That was good detective work," Benny told Henry.

"Thanks, but everyone helped." Henry sighed. "It didn't stop the oil spill though."

"No, but at least we know what happened," Jessie said. "Mr. Williams will be glad to know. The tugboat captain will be glad too."

"You're right," Henry said. "We can celebrate solving the mystery. Come on. Let's see what else we can do to help."

CHAPTER 10

A Change for the Better

For the rest of the week, the Aldens helped clean up at the beach, taking breaks to tour the Port Elizabeth area with Grandfather. The tugboat was towed to shore and raised up for repairs. The jagged hole could be fixed. Linda Tanaka looked happier now that she knew how the accident had happened. She'd be back to work in a few weeks.

On the Aldens' last day in Port Elizabeth, Jessie helped Mr. Young make French toast. Violet set the table, and Henry filled glasses with juice. Benny jumped into his chair and held up his knife and fork. He was ready to eat!

Grandfather and Kayla came in from the living room, where they had been up early talking. Everyone settled around the table and started breakfast one last time.

"Where do we go for cleanup today?" Henry asked. "We finished the part of the beach you gave us."

"The beach cleanup is done for now," Kayla said. "We've had lots of volunteers. Everyone did their share. It won't stay clean forever, of course. Trash will still wash in from the ocean. People will still drop garbage, but I think people are starting to understand the importance of keeping our beaches clean."

"Why do people do that—dump their trash?" Violet asked. "It's not that hard to find a garbage can."

Kayla shrugged. "I like to think it's an accident sometimes. They don't notice they dropped something or it falls out of a pocket or bag."

"I guess that means we'll always have a chance to help clean up," Henry said.

Mr. Young poured himself more coffee. "I always take an empty bag when I walk on the beach. I find a few pieces of trash every time. I pick them up to keep the beach looking nice."

"We could do that anywhere!" Jessie said. "At a park. In a neighborhood. Every walk would be a chance to help the planet."

"Good idea," Henry said. "We'll have to do that. But what about today? You must have some work we can do."

Violet nodded. "I'm not ready to stop. Too many animals need our help."

"I'm going to have one more piece of French toast," Benny said. "*Then* I'll be ready to help too!"

Kayla laughed. "You children have done plenty. Today, I have a surprise for you. Finish your breakfast and get ready to take a walk."

They washed the dishes and brushed their teeth.

They put on sunscreen and grabbed hats. The sun shone in a blue sky. A nice breeze off the ocean kept the air cool.

After a few minutes of walking, they reached some familiar dunes on the beach. "We're near the place where the piping plovers were nesting," Violet said.

"That's right. Let's go around the restricted area." Kayla led the way.

"Oh, you fixed the sign." Henry tried to wiggle the sign, and it wouldn't move. "It's very sturdy now."

"No more blowing over in the wind," Kayla said. "What else do you see?"

The Alden children looked at the sand dunes. This time they noticed how the breeze caused the grasses to wave. They noticed the small insects flying among the weeds and the tiny, plump bees landing on the flowers.

"Wait, what's that sound?" Jessie asked.

"It's the birds!" Violet bounced with excitement. "The plovers are back. See them?"

"I see one. There!" Benny pointed as a small bird

ran forward. It stopped and pecked at the ground. "Where's the other one?" Benny asked.

Kayla grinned. "The female is on a nest. The pair came back. Now they have four eggs!"

"Hooray!" Jessie cheered. "That's so exciting. Soon they'll have cute little babies, and maybe someday they won't be endangered."

"Every new chick helps," Kayla said.

"This must mean the beach is getting healthier," Henry said. He turned to Grandfather to explain. "The piping plover is an indicator species. If they are here that indicates a healthy beach."

"It's a good sign," Kayla said. "However, the beach isn't perfect. The effects of the oil spill will be felt for a very long time."

"At least we helped clean up the beach." Violet sighed. "I wish we could save all the endangered animals."

"I wish that too," Kayla said. "We have a lot of work ahead."

"It's a big job." Henry watched the orange-beaked

plover. They'd helped solve this one problem. That made him feel good. He also knew that they could keep making small changes every day to help the world.

"You've learned a lot," Kayla said. "I'm impressed with what you know."

"We learned about new animals," Henry said.

"And about protecting habitats," Violet added.

"We learned how to wash oil off animals," Jessie said.

"And that mayonnaise makes turtles poop!" Benny said.

Grandfather laughed. "I'm impressed with my grandchildren. You've done so much to help out. In fact, Kayla and I have been talking. Isn't that right, Kayla?"

Kayla nodded. "How would you like to join me on my travels? We'll visit different habitats—some of them very far away. You'll learn about different animals. Are you up for that?"

"Will we be able to help the animals?" Violet asked.

"Absolutely!" Kayla said. "That's a big part of the job."

"Can we really, Grandfather?" Jessie asked.

"Why not?" He winked. "After all, it's educational. Benny wanted to travel far and wide and see endangered animals. I can't think of a better way than traveling with Kayla. Think of all you'll learn."

"Hooray!" Benny cheered. "I get to go help animals all over the world! We all do!"

Henry grinned at Kayla. "I think you have our answer," he said. "Yes, please!"

Turn the page for a sneak preview of

Mystery of the Spotted Leopard

the next book in the
Endangered Animals series.

"I can't wait to see the real thing," said Violet, adding spots to the drawing in her sketchpad. "I'll draw an even better one then."

"I'd say your snow leopards look pretty good already," Henry said from across the airplane aisle. Then he turned back to the book about India he was reading to his little brother, Benny.

Henry was the oldest of the four Alden children. He was used to watching out for the others. On this trip, he had a lot of responsibility. The children were on a flight halfway around the world. Until they landed, he was in charge. And with Benny, that meant making sure he didn't get too antsy.

Jessie reviewed the notes she'd written in her notebook. She liked to keep the children's travels organized. "We will land in Leh," she said. "That is the largest city in Ladakh."

"Huh?" said Benny. "I thought we were going to India."

"Ladakh is a territory in India," Jessie explained. "It's in the northern part of the country. It's also one of the highest up places in the world."

Henry nodded. "A perfect place for snow leopards," he said. "They live far up in the mountains. And the Himalayas have the highest peaks anywhere."

A voice came over the airplane's speakers announcing that they would be landing soon. Violet closed her sketchpad. Jessie tucked her notebook into her backpack. Henry put away the book he was reading and made sure everyone had their seatbelts on.

Benny bounced in his seat. "I can't wait to see Kayla again!"

Kayla had been so impressed with the Aldens' help in Port Elizabeth, she'd invited them to come along as she helped protect other animals around the world.

Benny gazed out the window as the plane descended. They'd been flying above clouds. Now mountain ranges stretched as far as he could see. The tops of the mountains were white with snow.

"Everything is so big," said Benny. "It must be hard to find snow leopards in the mountains."

Violet leaned over to look. "I bet they can go all kinds of places people can't. They probably hide well too."

"That's why Kayla and PAW need to study them," Jessie said. "PAW wants to find out how snow leopards act in the wild. They also want to know how people are affecting the cats."

Benny looked up at his big sister. "What do you mean? I like to pet cats and hear them purr."

Jessie grinned. "Don't try to pet a snow leopard. They're wild animals."

"I know," Benny said. "We shouldn't touch wild animals. We might hurt them, or they might hurt us."

"Right," said Henry. "I don't think you'll have a chance to touch a snow leopard anyway. They won't want to get close to us. But maybe we'll see one, if we're lucky."

Violet sighed. "I sure hope so. It would be sad to come all this way and never see a snow leopard."

"It will still be fun," Benny said. "We get to be in the mountains. Grandfather said it's really far from everything. It will be like living in the boxcar again."

Jessie chuckled. "Benny, the Himalayan wilderness might be a little tougher than the forests of Greenfield, Connecticut."

They watched as the plane lowered into a wide valley. A blue-gray river wound between green trees. Buildings came into view.

Before long, the plane touched down. Benny giggled as the plane bounced on the runway and slowed to a stop. When the plane reached the gate, a flight attendant escorted the children off the plane.

Finally, after hours of travel, the Aldens saw a friendly face. Kayla had big, smiling brown eyes, and her short hair bounced as she hurried over to greet them with hugs. She'd already been in India for a week and had traveled down from the PAW research center in the mountains to pick up the children.

Once everyone was ready, the Aldens followed Kayla outside, where a shuttle was waiting to pick them up. Benny yawned. "What time is it? It's bright out, but I feel like it's the middle of the night."

"We traveled a long time," Henry said. "Back home, it would be the middle of the night."

"You're also at a very high altitude," Kayla said. "Here we're more than eleven thousand feet up. The tallest mountain in New England isn't much higher than six thousand feet."

Jessie looked at the mountains rising in the distance. "And we aren't even to our final destination yet."

"No," said Kayla, "but the air is thinner at this height. It has less oxygen in it, which makes it harder to breathe. We'll rest here in Leh to get used to the altitude. Then we'll go to the research center farther up."

Violet took a deep breath. "Does that mean even less air?" she asked.

Kayla put an arm around Violet's shoulders. "It does. But don't worry, we'll take it slow. Plus, you kids are in good shape. I saw the way you ran around the beach back in Port Elizabeth."

After a short shuttle ride, the Aldens reached the hotel and took their bags to their rooms. Once they were settled in, they could really feel the effects of the long flight. The children climbed into comfy beds, and one by one, they fell asleep. A new adventure was about to begin, and if they were going to succeed in spotting a snow leopard, they needed to be rested for it.

THE BOXCAR CHILDREN® MYSTERIES

THE BOXCAR CHILDREN
SURPRISE ISLAND
THE YELLOW HOUSE MYSTERY
MYSTERY RANCH
MIKE'S MYSTERY
BLUE BAY MYSTERY
THE WOODSHED MYSTERY
THE LIGHTHOUSE MYSTERY
MOUNTAIN TOP MYSTERY
SCHOOLHOUSE MYSTERY
CABOOSE MYSTERY
HOUSEBOAT MYSTERY
SNOWBOUND MYSTERY
TREE HOUSE MYSTERY
BICYCLE MYSTERY
MYSTERY IN THE SAND
MYSTERY BEHIND THE WALL
BUS STATION MYSTERY
BENNY UNCOVERS A MYSTERY
THE HAUNTED CABIN MYSTERY
THE DESERTED LIBRARY MYSTERY
THE ANIMAL SHELTER MYSTERY
THE OLD MOTEL MYSTERY
THE MYSTERY OF THE HIDDEN PAINTING
THE AMUSEMENT PARK MYSTERY
THE MYSTERY OF THE MIXED-UP ZOO
THE CAMP-OUT MYSTERY
THE MYSTERY GIRL
THE MYSTERY CRUISE
THE DISAPPEARING FRIEND MYSTERY
THE MYSTERY OF THE SINGING GHOST
THE MYSTERY IN THE SNOW
THE PIZZA MYSTERY
THE MYSTERY HORSE
THE MYSTERY AT THE DOG SHOW
THE CASTLE MYSTERY
THE MYSTERY OF THE LOST VILLAGE
THE MYSTERY ON THE ICE
THE MYSTERY OF THE PURPLE POOL
THE GHOST SHIP MYSTERY
THE MYSTERY IN WASHINGTON, DC
THE CANOE TRIP MYSTERY
THE MYSTERY OF THE HIDDEN BEACH
THE MYSTERY OF THE MISSING CAT
THE MYSTERY AT SNOWFLAKE INN

THE MYSTERY ON STAGE
THE DINOSAUR MYSTERY
THE MYSTERY OF THE STOLEN MUSIC
THE MYSTERY AT THE BALL PARK
THE CHOCOLATE SUNDAE MYSTERY
THE MYSTERY OF THE HOT AIR BALLOON
THE MYSTERY BOOKSTORE
THE PILGRIM VILLAGE MYSTERY
THE MYSTERY OF THE STOLEN BOXCAR
THE MYSTERY IN THE CAVE
THE MYSTERY ON THE TRAIN
THE MYSTERY AT THE FAIR
THE MYSTERY OF THE LOST MINE
THE GUIDE DOG MYSTERY
THE HURRICANE MYSTERY
THE PET SHOP MYSTERY
THE MYSTERY OF THE SECRET MESSAGE
THE FIREHOUSE MYSTERY
THE MYSTERY IN SAN FRANCISCO
THE NIAGARA FALLS MYSTERY
THE MYSTERY AT THE ALAMO
THE OUTER SPACE MYSTERY
THE SOCCER MYSTERY
THE MYSTERY IN THE OLD ATTIC
THE GROWLING BEAR MYSTERY
THE MYSTERY OF THE LAKE MONSTER
THE MYSTERY AT PEACOCK HALL
THE WINDY CITY MYSTERY
THE BLACK PEARL MYSTERY
THE CEREAL BOX MYSTERY
THE PANTHER MYSTERY
THE MYSTERY OF THE QUEEN'S JEWELS
THE STOLEN SWORD MYSTERY
THE BASKETBALL MYSTERY
THE MOVIE STAR MYSTERY
THE MYSTERY OF THE PIRATE'S MAP
THE GHOST TOWN MYSTERY
THE MYSTERY OF THE BLACK RAVEN
THE MYSTERY IN THE MALL
THE MYSTERY IN NEW YORK
THE GYMNASTICS MYSTERY
THE POISON FROG MYSTERY
THE MYSTERY OF THE EMPTY SAFE
THE HOME RUN MYSTERY
THE GREAT BICYCLE RACE MYSTERY

GERTRUDE CHANDLER WARNER discovered when she was teaching that many readers who like an exciting story could find no books that were both easy and fun to read. She decided to try to meet this need, and her first book, *The Boxcar Children*, quickly proved she had succeeded.

Miss Warner drew on her own experiences to write the mystery. As a child she spent hours watching trains go by on the tracks opposite her family home. She often dreamed about what it would be like to set up housekeeping in a caboose or freight car—the situation the Alden children find themselves in.

While the mystery element is central to each of Miss Warner's books, she never thought of them as strictly juvenile mysteries. She liked to stress the Aldens' independence and resourcefulness and their solid New England devotion to using up and making do. The Aldens go about most of their adventures with as little adult supervision as possible—something else that delights young readers.

Miss Warner lived in Putnam, Connecticut, until her death in 1979. During her lifetime, she received hundreds of letters from girls and boys telling her how much they liked her books.